DATE DUE

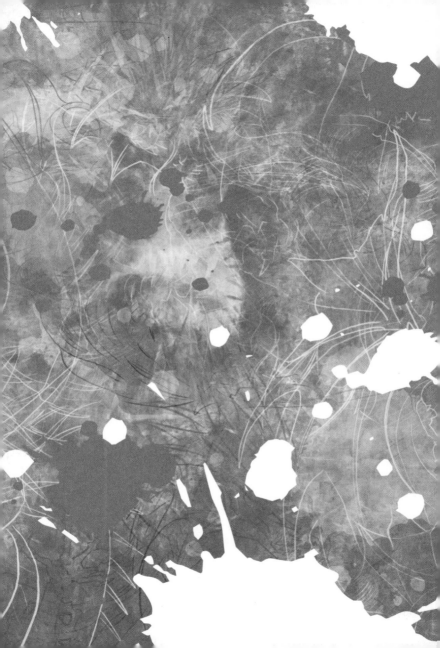

DRAGONBLOOD

DRAGON THEFT AUTO

Michael Dahl

Yap Kun Rong

STONE ARCH BOOKS
www.stonearchbooks.com

Zone Books are published by
Stone Arch Books
151 Good Counsel Drive, P.O. Box 669
Mankato, Minnesota 56002
www.stonearchbooks.com

Library of Congress Cataloging-in-Publication Data
Dahl, Michael.
    Dragon Theft Auto / by Michael Dahl; illustrated by
Yap Kun Rong.
    p. cm. — (Zone Books. Dragonblood)
    ISBN 978-1-4342-1264-1 (library binding)
    [1. Dragons—Fiction. 2. Automobile theft—Fiction.
3. Friendship—Fiction.] I. Kun Rong, Yap, ill. II. Title.
PZ7.D15134Drt 2009
[Fic]—dc22   2008031281

Summary: Sixteen-year-old Henry travels to a strange
city in search of his missing friend. Someone, or
something, in the city is stealing cars. Is the missing
boy mixed up with the crime? Henry thinks something
bigger is behind the thefts. Something with wings.

Creative Director: Heather Kindseth
Graphic Designer: Brann Garvey

1 2 3 4 5 6 14 13 12 11 10 09

TABLE OF CONTENTS

Introduction

A new Age of Dragons is about to begin. The **powerful** creatures will return to rule the **world** once more, but this time will be **different.** This time, they will have allies. Who will **help** them? Around the world, some young humans are making a strange **discovery.** They are learning that they were born with **dragon blood** – blood that gives them **amazing powers.**

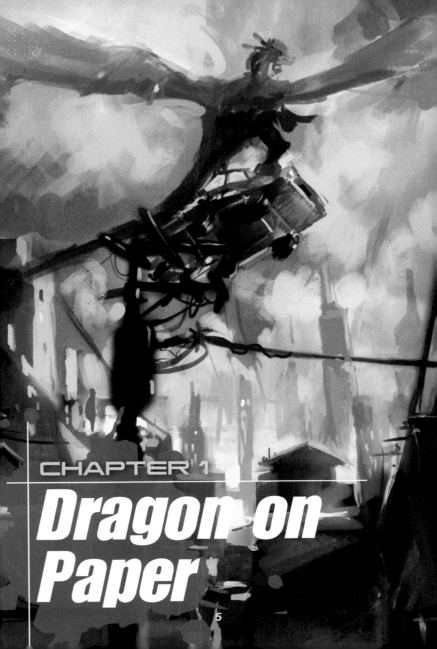

CHAPTER 1

Dragon on
Paper

A young man named Henry sat on a bus, drawing a picture.

"Hey man, what's that?" asked another passenger.

"Um, it's nothing," said the young man.

The passenger grabbed the pad of paper away from Henry.

HA! HA!

He stared at the picture and *laughed*.

"Is this what you think is happening to all those stolen cars?" asked the man.

Henry shrugged.

The man returned the pad to Henry.

"Well, who knows?" said the man. "Your guess is as good as anyone else's."

CHAPTER 2
Missing Cars

Henry got off the bus at the next stop.

The buildings were dark.

The *streetlights* flickered on and off.

Henry had not been in this part of the city before.

A *breeze* blew a dirty
newspaper against his legs.

He reached down and grabbed
the paper.

The headlines were about the
car thieves again.

All over the city, cars were

disappearing.

No one knew how it was done,
or who the thieves were.

Henry had been having dreams
about the disappearing cars.

In his dreams, a strange flying creature grabbed them.

But Henry had come to the city searching for something else.

Something that was missing.

He was not looking for the lost cars.

Henry was looking for his friend.

CHAPTER 3
Blood Brothers

Last summer, Henry and his friend Matt became blood brothers.

Henry had seen it done on a TV show.

He and Matt both pricked their thumbs with a needle.

Bright blood appeared.

Then they touched thumbs and shook hands.

"We're **blood** brothers now," said Matt.

"Brothers forever," said Henry.

Matt's mother walked by the door to his room.

She saw the blood and screamed.

"What do you boys think you're doing?" she yelled.

"Blood can be dangerous!" she cried.

"People get sick from other people's blood," she added.

"We're blood brothers now," explained Matt.

Henry had to leave. Matt was grounded for the rest of the week.

For the rest of the summer, the two boys didn't see each other.

CHAPTER 4

Rooftops

Now, Henry stared down at his pad of paper.

Henry had a strange feeling.

He was sure that Matt was somewhere in the city.

He was also sure that his dream held a clue to finding his friend.

Henry stared at the picture again. Then he *looked* up.

High above him, the building's roof had a strange antenna.

It was the same antenna from his picture.

It was the same antenna he had seen in his dreams.

Henry found a 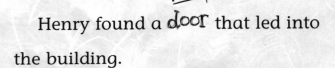door that led into the building.

He climbed a set of steep stairs.

Minutes later, Henry opened a rusty, metal door.

He was standing on the top of the building.

CHAPTER 5
The Nest

A huge pile of smashed cars lay on the roof.

These are the missing cars, thought Henry.

Just then, a **huge** shape rose up from the cars.

It shook its wings and yawned.

Henry stared at the **dragon.**

Its *yellow eyes* blinked at Henry.

The creature opened its jaws and
screamed.

Henry dropped his pad of paper.

His body trembled.

Wings began to sprout from his shoulders.

Soon there were two **dragons** on the rooftop.

They stood facing each other.

They each lifted a claw and then pressed them together.

The two dragons flapped their wings and flew into the gray sky.

Brothers forever.

Of Dragons and Near-Dragons

Lizards are a common sight in cities, as well as in deserts and jungles. Asian house geckos are common in houses and hotels. They walk on walls and ceilings. Green iguanas can be found on rooftops and on the side of roads.

Mediterranean geckos are widespread in parts of Texas. They can be found around homes and other buildings. This same species lives in Oklahoma, Arizona, Mexico, and the Caribbean.

The black spitting cobra can be found in the urban areas of Singapore. The snake hunts at night, eating pesky mice and rats. Sometimes, the cobra even slithers inside peoples' houses!

Australian cities have the biggest residential lizards in the world. Lizards around 23 inches (60 centimeters) long are a common sight in gardens and backyards. Luckily, there are no poisonous lizards in Australia.

The northern curly-tailed lizard has made its home in southern Florida. This creature can be found at strip malls, parking lots, and many other places around town. It is called the "T. rex of ground lizards," and likes to snuggle up against warm cement.

ABOUT THE AUTHOR

Michael Dahl is the author of more than 200 books for children and young adults. He has won the AEP Distinguished Achievement Award three times for his nonfiction. His Finnegan Zwake mystery series was shortlisted twice by the Anthony and Agatha awards. He has also written the *Library of Doom* series. He is a featured speaker at conferences around the country on graphic novels and high-interest books for boys.

ABOUT THE ILLUSTRATOR

Yap Kun Rong is a freelance illustrator and concept artist for books, comics, and video games. He lives and works in Tokyo, Japan.

GLOSSARY

allies (AL-eyez)—people or countries that give support to each other

creature (KREE-chur)—a living thing that is human or animal

dangerous (DAYN-jur-uhss)—likely to cause harm or injury

flickered (FLIK-urd)—blinked or moved unsteadily

passenger (PASS-uhn-jur)—someone besides the driver who travels in a car or other vehicle

pricked (PRIKD)—made a small hole

rule (ROOL)—have power over something

sprout (SPROUT)—to grow, appear, or develop quickly

steep (STEEP)—very high

DISCUSSION QUESTIONS

1. Was it right for the man on the bus to grab Henry's drawing? Have you ever been in a similar situation?

2. Why did Matt's mom get so angry when Matt and Henry became blood brothers?

3. Was Matt or Henry the original dragon? Explain your reasons.

WRITING PROMPTS

1. Henry had a very detailed dream. Write about your favorite dream.

2. What did you think was happening to all of the cars that were disappearing? Write three different explanations for the missing cars.

3. At the end of the story, Matt and Henry fly off together. But is that really the end? Write another chapter to the book describing where Matt and Henry go.

INTERNET SITES

The book may be over, but the adventure is just beginning.

Do you want to read more about the subjects or ideas in this book? Want to play cool games or watch videos about the authors who write these books? Then go to FactHound. At *www.facthound.com,* you'll be able to do all that, and more. The FactHound website can also send you to other safe Internet sites.

Check it out!